This book has been presented to:

_____

And was first read to them by:

_____

D1501527

The Reading Pig
Goes to Music Class

Author— Nicholas I. Clement

Illustrator—Judy Nostrant

Teachers
Change Brains
media

The Reading Pig Goes to Music Class. Copyright ©2019 by Nicholas I. Clement Ed. D.
Teachers Change Brains Media. All rights reserved.
Printed in the Unites States of America. No part of this book shall be used or reproduced in any manner whatsoever without written
permission except in the case of brief quotations embodied in critical articles and reviews.

Teachers Change Brains Media books may be purchased for educational, business or sales promotional use.
For information – www.thereadingpig.com
Library of Congress Cataloging in Publication Data is available on request.

ISBN – 9780996389181 First edition. July 2018

Book management & marketing services – www.maxfemurmedia.com

Illustrations – Judy Nostrant

Cover layout & pre-press production — Pattie Copenhaver

Acknowledgements -

First, The Reading Pig went to school to help Dr. C inspire students to read. The Reading Pig had so much fun, the next adventure was to Mrs. Klinkingbeard's school library. Then, The Reading Pig was the guest of Miss Jessica's students on a field trip to the desert. Thanks to the following partners and generous donors, The Reading Pig was able to experience the magic of music as he tagged along with Amanda and Cole to music class.

Emily Meschter, DHL- In 2012, Emily Meschter was awarded an Honorary Doctor of Humane Letters Degree by the University of Arizona, College of Education for her long and distinguished career as a philanthropist and supporter of education extraordinaire. In 2010, the Flowing Wells Unified School District honored Emily for her incredible contributions to the district by creating the Emily Meschter Early Learning Center. The Reading Pig adventures continue because of Emily's strong belief in the power of early childhood literacy.

Judy Nostrant, Illustrator- Judy captured the excitement of school from the first Reading Pig cover and continues to amaze and delight readers, young and old, with her illustrations.

Pattie Copenhaver, Graphic Designer- Pattie makes The Reading Pig Goes to Music Class book easy to read and has created a series often found on children's "read it to me every night" list.

Jennifer Anglin, Editor- Jennifer is an invaluable member of the publishing team. Her editing skills are incredible and help The Reading Pig series model effective writing skills for future young authors.

Tim Derrig, Book Manager- Tim handles all the details, big, small and everything in-between. His passion for The Reading Pig project is larger than life.

Northern Arizona University- As a university partner, NAU continues to support children's literacy through sponsorship at the Tucson Festival of Books.

Pima Federal Credit Union and Simply Bits- A generous grant from PFCU brought The Reading Pig to life in 2016. Simply Bits continues to support The Reading Pig project by developing and maintaining thereadingpig.com

Music Teachers- A shout out to all the music teachers in the world. You bring joy and happiness to all. Just check out the smile on Amanda, Cole and Isabella faces!

We are grateful for your collective efforts and support,
Nic aka "Dr. C"

Dedicated to
My Father, William Clement

Your love of music and life in general, lives on!

University of Michigan Marching Band

1935 - 36
Fourth Year Cornet

© 2019   Nicholas I. Clement
ISBN: 9780996389181
Published by:
Teachers Change Brains Media

legendaryteacher.com

The Reading Pig Goes to Music Class

Every time we open a new book, we get to go on an exciting adventure!
When we dive into a story, we become part of its magic. Stories can make
us laugh. Stories connect us with each other. Stories make us curious.
They help us imagine, learn, and discover. When you read every day,
you grow your mind. You also inspire your heart because stories
can fuel dreams.

In this story, the Reading Pig makes a fantastic journey to music class.
Amanda, Cole and their friends are excited to learn to make music.
When we listen to stories, the words also make their own kind of music.
This story has many wonderful words that dance off the pages! It includes
one of my most favorite words: awe. This special word means to be amazed.
Awe means our eyes are wide with excitement! Awe means to be filled
with wonder. I hope this story fills you with the wonder and joy of reading.

Thank you Dr. C for creating another delightful Reading Pig adventure to
inspire our young readers.

Happy reading!
Jenny Volpe

Jenny Volpe is CEO of Make Way for Books, an early childhood literacy nonprofit
organization dedicated to helping children fall in love with books and reading.

makewayforbooks.com

Enjoy the tale...

Hi, my name is Amanda.
I want to tell you my story.
It was Tuesday. We go to
music class on Tuesday.
We are learning to play all
kinds of musical
instruments! My favorite
is the recorder.
Mr. B is our teacher.
He told us we would have
a guest conductor visit our
class today.
We were **curious**.

I looked at our job chart. It was my turn to be line leader. Cole was the caboose.

JOB CHART

line leader	Amanda
line caboose	Cole
pencils	Maria
lights	Jose
papers	Viggo

We got out of our seats and formed a very straight line.

Mr. B came into the class and greeted us. He asked if we were ready for music class. We all said yes at the same time. He said that was music to his ears. We **laughed!**

Before we left class Cole raised his hand. Mr. B called on Cole, and he asked if we could take our Reading Pig to music class. Dr. C had given us his Reading Pig to remind us to read every day.

Cole asked if our Reading Pig could help us learn to read music? Mr. B said yes. We were **pleased.**

Cole let me hold the Reading Pig!

ONE TWO   ONE TWO   ONE TWO

Mr. B told us that we were going to march to
music class in honor of our guest conductor.
He showed us how to march.
We practiced marching in place.

ONE TWO   ONE TWO   ONE TWO

Mr. B clapped and we marched.

We had **rhythm**.

We went out the door.

I held up the Reading Pig high for everyone to see. Mr. B started clapping a little faster. We marched a little faster all the way to the music room.

We were tired. We sat on the floor and rested. Mr. B gave us a choice of instruments.

He handed out cymbals.

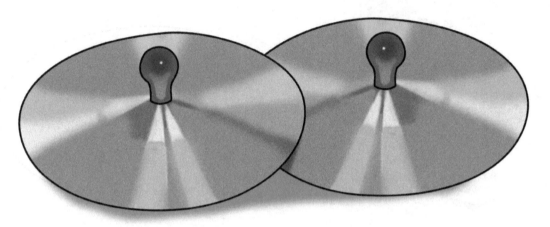

He handed out a drum and drumsticks.

He handed out a triangle.
We could not wait to make
music. We were **excited**.
I picked my favorite.
I picked a recorder.

Mr. B then asked Cole which instrument he wanted to play. Cole said he wanted to play the Reading Pig.
Mr. B was **puzzled.**

CRASH

Mr. B taught us to warm
up our instruments. He
had each one of us play
our instrument.
Crash went the cymbals!

Bang went the drum.

Ting went the triangle.

Tweet went my recorder.

Can you guess what sound the Reading Pig made? **Wop** went the Reading Pig. Mr. B laughed!

Now he wanted us to play our instruments together. Mr B clapped five times and we played with each clap.

CRASH
CRASH
CRASH
CRASH
CRASH

BANG
BANG
BANG
BANG
BANG

TING
TING
TING
TING
TING

WOP
WOP
WOP
WOP
WOP

TWEET
TWEET
TWEET
TWEET
TWEET

Mr. B then taught us a fun game.
He had all the instruments on
a table in front of the class.
He pointed to an
instrument.

We played that instrument

TWEET

until he pointed to another.

Ting, Wop, Bang,Crash. Then he went faster.

Bang, Ting, Tweet, Crash, Wop.

There was a knock at the door. Mr. B gave us the quiet signal. He said our special guest conductor was here. We were fired up! Mr. B opened the door and introduced our special guest conductor, Isabella. Isabella was the Drum Major with the high school band. She had the tallest hat I had ever seen, with a black strap under her chin. Her uniform was dark blue and sparkling gold with glistening silver buttons. Her black shoes were so shiny that we could see our reflections. She carried a long baton with a crown on top. We were in **awe**.

Isabella told us that she was the leader of the high school marching band. She told us how she started playing the recorder in Mr. B's music class. She told us how great band is because you get to wear this cool uniform. She told us how much fun it is to march in parades. She was **enthusiastic.**

Mr. B said we were in for an extraordinary treat. Isabella was going to be our Drum Major. We all formed our line. I was line leader and Cole was the caboose. We took our instruments. We were **prepared**. Drum Major Isabella told us to march and play our instruments as she moved her baton up and down.

WOP
WOP

TING
TING

CRASH
CRASH

We followed Drum Major Isabella out the door and around the school. We made a parade!

BANG BANG

TWEET TWEET

Dr. C was visiting the school. He watched us march and clapped loudly. We marched in a circle playing our instruments.

Drum Major Isabella gave us the signal to stop
in front of Dr. C. We gave her our **attention.**

Dr. C told us he was very excited to see our marching band. Dr. C told Drum Major Isabella how proud he was of her. He asked each of us to play our instruments. We were **loud**!

Dr. C clapped and then looked **puzzled**. He asked what happened to the **wop** sound? I said the Reading Pig made that sound and he had disappeared. We were **smiling.**

Dr. C said he needed his Reading Pig to take to another school. We told Dr. C to say oink three times. Dr. C said **"Oink, Oink, Oink."** Nothing happened. He looked **sad.**

We told Dr. C to say **"Oink"** three times again, but louder. As loud as a marching band. Dr. C roared

"Oink, Oink, Oink!"

Drum Major Isabella lifted her tall, tall hat. There was the Reading Pig!

We all played our instruments at the same time.

BANG TING CRASH WOP TWEET

We love music class and the Reading Pig!

The End

CPSIA information can be obtained
at www.ICGtesting.com
Printed in the USA
BVHW011636151119
563880BV00020BA/1/P